The Token Gift

The
Token
Gift

Story by
Hugh William McKibbon

Illustrations by
Scott Cameron

Annick Press Ltd. • Toronto • New York

Second printing, February 1998

Annick Press Ltd.

We acknowledge the support of the Canada Council for the Arts for our publishing program.
We also thank the Ontario Arts Council.

The publishers wish to express their deep appreciation to Sally Bryer Mennell for her editorial contribution.

The author would like to thank Ravi Ravindra, Cynthia Taylor and Christopher Reardon for their invaluable help and advice.

The artist would like to thank Beth Knox of The Royal Ontario Museum for being so generous with her time and expertise.

Cataloguing in Publication Data
  McKibbon, Hugh William
    The token gift

  ISBN 1-55037-499-0 (bound) ISBN 1-55037-498-2 (pbk.)

  I. Cameron, Scott (Scott R.). II. Title.

  PS8575.K52T6 1996   jC813'.54   C96-930148-0
  PZ7.M35TO 1996

The art in this book was rendered in oils.
The text was typeset in Garamond condensed.

Distributed in Canada by:
Firefly Books Ltd.
3680 Victoria Park Avenue
Willowdale, ON
M2H 3K1

Published in the U.S.A. by Annick Press (U.S.) Ltd.
Distributed in the U.S.A. by:
Firefly Books (U.S.) Inc.
P.O. Box 1338
Ellicott Station
Buffalo, NY 14205

Printed and bound in Canada by
Friesens, Altona, Manitoba.

To my remarkable 89-year-old mother, Margaret, who once bested a roomful of mathematical "experts" by instantly and easily answering the following brain-teasing question: What is the next letter in the sequence O.T.T.F.F.S.S....?
—H.W.M.

For Johanna
—S.C.

Long ago, in India, an old man lived in a castle with many turrets and spires, overlooking the sea. He was very wealthy and generous. The people in the region loved him and gave him the title *Rajrishi*, "wise one", to honour his leadership. He had a beautiful and intelligent wife, and many fine children.

But the Rajrishi was not satisfied. His children had grown and left home. His body was old and his joints were stiff. His days were long and unexciting. One day, feeling quite useless, he exclaimed to his wife, "If only I had been a king, I might have been able to do something great with my life!"

"And what would that have been?" she asked.

"Oh, I don't know. I would like to have made the world a better place," he replied dreamily.

"But you have, my dear!" she said. "Remember how you started."

And gazing out, over the sea, Mohan the Rajrishi remembered...

How he loved to play games! When he was young he would squat with his friends in the village square, throwing dice and moving stones or pieces of wood around on a playing board scratched in the dust. Their clothes were tattered and their feet were bare, but they played every day from sunup until dark. Mohan was the best at inventing new rules, and the games were constantly changing.

Gradually he began to think up an entirely new game.

From as long ago as he could remember, his grandfather, who had been in the army, had told him stories of war.

"The generals plotted it all out before a battle," Grandfather said. "They tried to decide where to place their men in order to win. They called this military strategy."

Mohan was fascinated. "We can make a game," he cried in excitement. "We can plan a battle, but no one will be killed. The pieces will be the army and the board the battlefield, and it will be a game of strategy!"

The game was played by four players on a board divided into sixty-four squares. He called it *Chaturanga*. The word came from Sanskrit, the ancient language spoken by the scholars, and meant "four divisions". The armies of India had four divisions—chariots, elephants, cavalry and infantry—so he made four pieces, each representing a division, and added two more pieces to represent a vizier and a king.

At first it was a game of chance. The players threw dice or flipped a coin to determine how the pieces would move and how one piece could "capture" another. "Roll a good one," they would shout to each other, and the games became very noisy and exciting, because anything could happen and anyone could win with just a twist of the dice.

Then Mohan changed the rules. There were no dice, and all the moves depended on strategy: how well one player could out-think the others. These games were silent and fierce as each player stared fixedly at the board. Some of Mohan's friends stopped playing.

"It is not fair," they said. "He is too clever. He always wins."

So Mohan decided to use a combination of luck and skill, and allowed the dice to determine the moves to keep the game exciting.

But he liked the game of strategy best, and finally settled on a version for only two players in which each had to think several moves ahead and try to trap the other's king. "*Shah mat*," was the winner's cry, "the king is trapped."

"Checkmate! The king has been defeated."

Mohan began to supply local storekeepers with his game. It was bought by military men, lawyers, scholars, and children in the village square. People gathered to play the game and analyze their strategies. Players travelled great distances to compete in Chaturanga contests. Mohan could not keep up with the demand. He built a workshop and hired crafts-people to make the boards and gamepieces. Word spread to other countries, and eventually Mohan built hundreds of workshops throughout India and hired thousands of workers to manufacture the games. He became very wealthy.

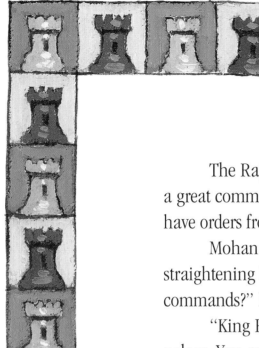

The Rajrishi's memories were interrupted by a great commotion. "I must see the Rajrishi. I have orders from King Raju."

Mohan stepped away from the window, straightening his robes. "What is it my king commands?" he asked the messenger.

"King Raju commands your presence at the palace. You are to come with me."

The Rajrishi felt suddenly younger, and his farewell to his wife was almost brisk.

The journey took several days. When they arrived at the palace, Mohan was shown to a splendid suite of rooms. After a brief rest he was escorted with great ceremony into the presence of King Raju.

"Rajrishi Mohan, your game has given me many hours of pleasure," the King said. "I have played since I was a small boy, and only recently did I learn that the inventor of Chaturanga was living right here, in my own kingdom."

The Rajrishi bowed.

"This game of yours has brought honour to our country," the King continued. "Our generals have learned strategies on your playing board that have helped us to win on the battlefield. I would like to reward you. What do you think would be a suitable reward?"

"Your Majesty, you are generous," Mohan replied, "but I am an old man and wealthy. I have no wants."

The King frowned. "Rajrishi Mohan, it is dishonourable to refuse a gift from your king," he said irritably. "I command you to choose a suitable reward."

Mohan thought carefully. In the very centre of the court, built into the floor, was a Chaturanga gameboard made up of sixty-four ceramic tiles. As his eye fell upon the gameboard he had an idea. He said, "Your Majesty, I ask only for a token. Give me one grain of rice to represent the first square of the Chaturanga board, two for the second, four for the third, eight for the fourth, and so on, doubling each time until all of the sixty-four squares have been accounted for."

Then the King made a mistake. "Is that all?" he asked. "That does not seem like much of a reward to me."

"It is all that I wish for, Your Majesty."

So the King sent for a bag of rice and ordered a servant to distribute it on the ceramic tiles of the gameboard according to the Rajrishi's request.

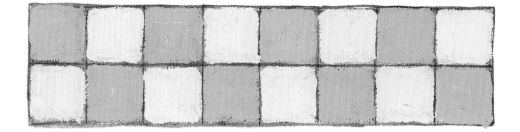

When the eighth square needed 128 grains of rice, the King sent for more servants to help with the counting.

After the first sixteen squares, the bag of rice was used up, except for one grain. In fact, the sixteenth square used *32,768 grains*—exactly one half of the bag. The King could see that the following square would use one whole bag and realized that there was not enough rice in the court.

"Bring an entire shipload of rice," he ordered.

Of course, the eighteenth square used two bags, the nineteenth used four bags, and so on. By the time they reached the thirty-second square, the entire shipload had been used, except for one grain. In fact, the thirty-second square by itself had used up 32,768 bags. Exactly one half of an average shipload.

By this time it was late in the night and the watchers in the court were weary. The King could see that something was seriously wrong. The thirty-third square alone would require one entire shipload.

Something had to be done.

He said, "It grows late. Let us all retire and in the morning I will consult the Royal Mathematician. Rest well."

But the King did not rest well. This request had seemed so simple, and yet...

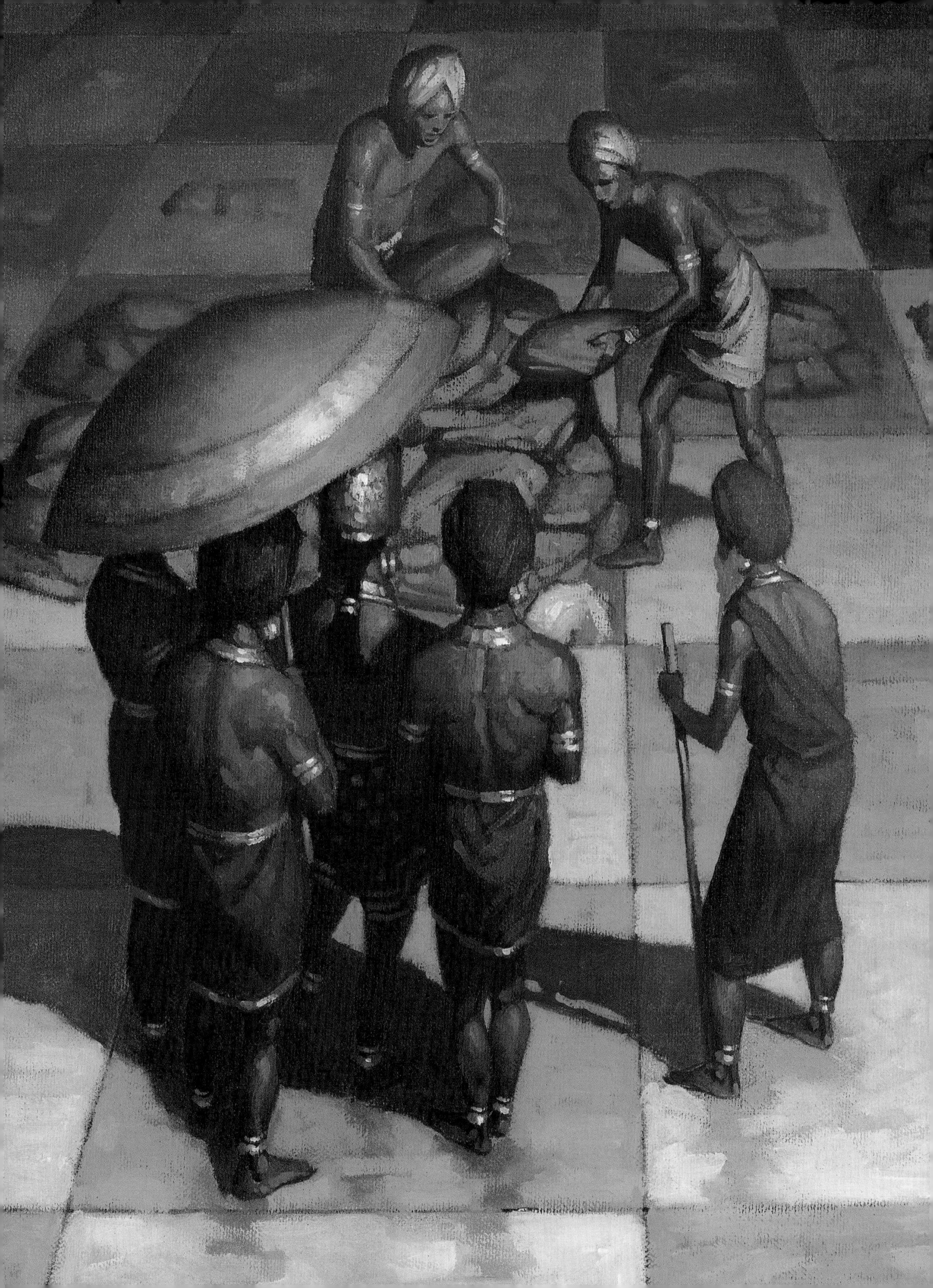

grains		bags		shiploads		years	
1	1	17	1	33	1	49	1
2	2	18	2	34	2	50	2
3	4	19	4	35	4	51	4
	8	20	8	36	8	52	8
	16	21	16	37	16	53	16
	32	22	32	38	32	54	32
	64	23	64	39	64	55	64
	128	24	128	40	128	56	128
	256	25	256	41	256	57	256
	512	26	512	42	512	58	512
	1,024	27	1,024	43	1,024	59	1,024
12	2,048	28	2,048	44	20,48	60	2,048
13	4,096	29	4,096	45	4,096	61	4,096
14	8,192	30	8,192	46	8,192	62	8,192
15	16384	31	16,384	47	16,384	63	16,384
16	32,768	32	32,768	48	32,768	64	32,768
total so far		total so far		total so far		final total	
65,536 -1 grain		65,536 bags -1 grain		65,536 shiploads -1 grain		65,536 years -1 grain	

In the morning the report from the Royal Mathematician was disturbing.

"Your Majesty," he said, drawing a chart on the wall, "watch what will happen as I fill in the numbers. As you can see, the forty-eighth square will require 32,768 shiploads, not to mention that all the squares before the forty-eighth will have required the same total sum. For the first forty-eight squares you will require 65,536 shiploads, and there will be only one grain left over!"

"Enough!" bellowed the King. "Send for the Royal Farm Advisor."

The Royal Farm Advisor was brought before the King. When told of the problem he said gloomily, "It will take half a year, not just for your kingdom, but for the whole world to grow 32,768 shiploads of rice."

Then the Royal Mathematician, who had completed his chart, said, "Your Majesty, I am afraid that the amount required for the forty-ninth square would take one full year to grow."

The King looked down the column to the last square, the sixty-fourth.

"But no! That means that the last square would require..."

"Yes, Your Majesty. It would require 32,768 years for the entire world to grow enough rice for the last square alone." The Royal Mathematician, who was very precise, as mathematicians are, continued, "In fact, to account for the whole board, Your Majesty, would take the world 65,536 years. There would be only one grain left over."

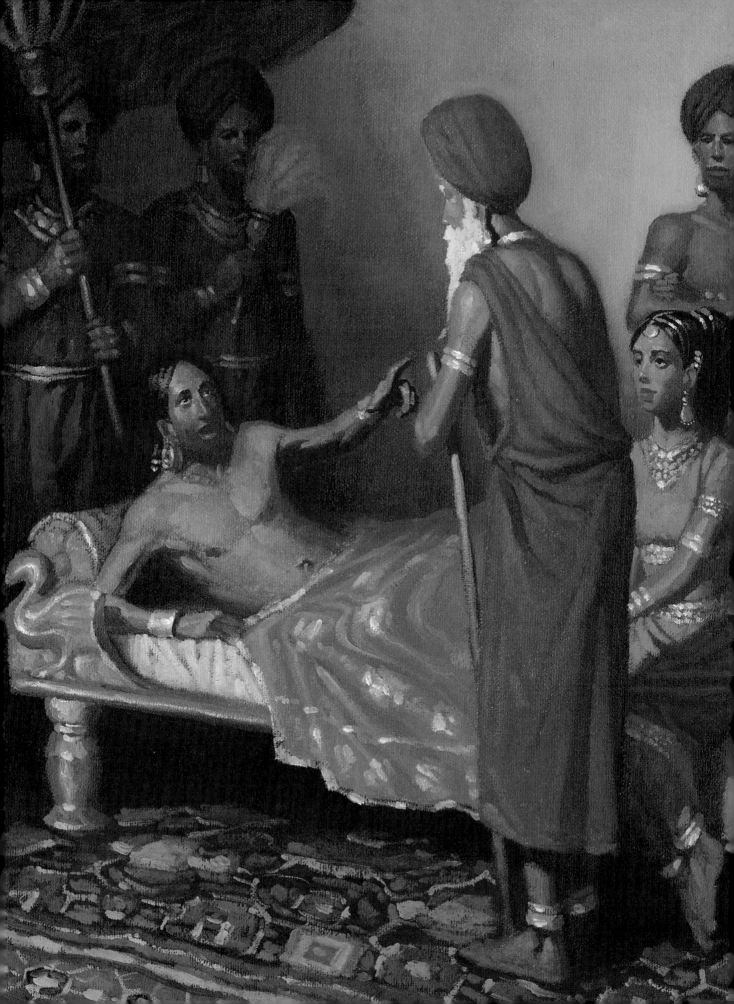

The Royal Historian said that, as agriculture had only been practised for about 10,000 years, too little rice had *ever* been grown to solve this problem.

King Raju knew that it would not be possible for him to keep his word. In this part of India it was considered most important for a person to keep his word, and particularly for a king to do so. A king who could not do what he promised was not worthy of being king.

Raju felt sick and took to his bed. He tossed and turned and no one could cure his fever. Eventually he sent for the Rajrishi.

"Rajrishi Mohan, you have proven yourself wiser than I am. You have put me in a difficult position. I cannot keep my word, so honour demands that I step down. I appoint you king from this moment."

Mohan could not believe his ears. Then he bowed deeply. "Thank you, Your Majesty."

He went to the throne room alone.

"I am a king," he said out loud to the empty room. "What shall I do now?"

His own voice echoed back at him. Everyone had left the chamber and the palace was silent.

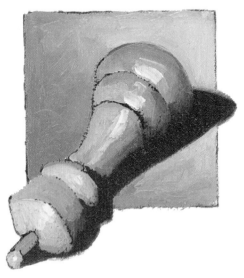

"If only my wife were here," he thought. "What was it she said? This is not the way I imagined it would feel to be the king."

He wandered around the palace, observing everything but speaking to no one. He felt let down; disappointed. Inside himself nothing had changed. He was still the same person he had always been. He returned to the throne and sat and thought and thought. Finally, as darkness fell, he arose and returned to Raju's bedside.

"Your Ex-Majesty," he said, "in my new position as king, here is my first...and only...decree. I hereby abdicate from the throne and reinstate you as king."

Raju was nonplussed. "But why?" he cried.

"Because I now see that I tricked you with cleverness," replied Mohan. "Cleverness is not enough. I believe that honour is a more important quality than cleverness, and you are a good and honourable man. This experience may make you even wiser: you have learned that things are not always as simple as they appear. It is the same with Chaturanga. I have given it much thought, and I now know that I do not need to be a king. In my way I have already given something to the world."

King Raju rewarded Rajrishi Mohan with a gold medal that he designed himself. Engraved on the front was the image of one grain of rice. On the back was the inscription, "He is a very special man who possesses both intelligence and honour." And below it was engraved "Rajrishi Mohan" and the date.

Mohan returned home to live the rest of his days a completely satisfied man. King Raju had a long and successful reign.

Chaturanga is now called chess, and it is played all over the world.

AFTERWORD

No one knows exactly how old the game of chess is, or exactly where it comes from. We do know that it was in existence by the sixth century A.D., and might go as far back as the fourth century B.C. This means that the game could be as much as 2400 years old. Historical evidence does strongly suggest that it was invented in India, somewhere near the Ganges river.

Chaturanga means "four divisions", and this probably meant military divisions; this has helped historians date the game by matching the playing pieces to the kind of soldiers and animals that were used in Indian warfare hundreds of years ago.

The legend that this book is based on helped the historians, too. It comes from Persia, but is set in India during the third dynasty B.C. A vizier* said to have invented the game of chess asked the king for grain as his reward, with the same catastrophic mathematical result as in our story. The human outcome is uncertain, but some versions of the story suggest that the vizier lost his head...literally!

Nobody knows, either, when chess changed from a four-person game involving elements of chance to the purely strategic game for only two players. By the sixth century it had spread to Persia, and it became popular throughout the Arab world. The game reached Europe in the tenth century through Arab contact with Spain and Sicily.

If you are interested in finding out more about the history of chess, visit your local bookstore or library.

* A vizier, or wazir, is an official high up in Muslim government.